Arthur Starter Book 09

ARTHUR'S
Homework

by Marc Brown

Long tail Books

Where We Live,
Elwood City
- Our Environment
- Our History
- Our Community
MATH

Brrriiinnng!

"Don't forget," called Mr. Ratburn. "Your Town Projects are due Friday!"

Arthur was a little worried. He didn't have an idea for his project yet. "I'll go right home and make a plan," he decided.

But the Brain tapped him on the shoulder.
"My project is studying wind patterns around Elwood City," said the Brain. "Could you help me out?"
"Um, okay," said Arthur.

TUCKER
PUT TRASH HERE

Before Arthur knew it, Monday afternoon was gone.

The next day, Arthur was just getting home from school when the phone rang.

"It's me," said Buster. "I'm making a video about Elwood City. Would you be my cameraman?"

"I guess so," said Arthur.

Before Arthur knew it, Tuesday afternoon was gone.

"Today is the day," said Arthur on Wednesday.
"I *have* to think of an idea for my project."

But after school Binky stopped by and asked Arthur to come to his house. He needed a hand with his History of Elwood City poster. A hand—and a body, too!

"You're a life saver," Binky told Arthur.

Before Arthur knew it, Wednesday afternoon was gone.

On Thursday, Arthur didn't even make it home for dinner.

"Help!" yelled Francine out her window. "I'm making a model of Elwood City, and it keeps falling apart!"

Westboro
APARTMENTS

Arthur mixed up pail after pail of plaster.
“It’s getting late,” he said. “And our projects are due tomorrow.”
“Don’t worry,” said Francine. “We’ll be done soon.”

Before Arthur knew it, Thursday afternoon was gone—
and most of Thursday evening, too.

Finally, Arthur got home. He sat down
to think of an idea for his own project.

He didn't get very far.

The next morning, everyone brought their Town Projects to class.
Everyone but Arthur.
"Where's your project, Arthur?" Mr. Ratburn asked.
Arthur didn't know what to say.

APRIL
Due Today
Your Town
Project

APRIL
TUCKER
SCHOOL
SUGAR BOWL
TOWN HALL
BANK
ELWOOD CITY

"Excuse me, Mr. Ratburn," said the Brain. "Arthur worked on my project. He was my partner."

"Mine, too," said Buster.

"And mine," said Binky.

"Don't forget me," said Francine.

"Wow, Arthur!" said Mr. Ratburn. "I see you've been very busy—with not just one project, but four!"

APRIL
Due Today:
Your Town
Project

"And four great friends, too!" said Arthur.